ZOOM

THROUGH

DOOM

ASHOK MALLI

Zoom through Doom
Copyright © 2022 by Ashok Malli

ISBN
978-1-956529-87-6 (Hardcover)
978-1-956529-62-3 (Paperback)
978-1-956529-61-6 (eBook)

Table of Contents

Characters

Prof Krishna Kumar is a Retired History Professor

Ms Erika Trompkova . . . Professor's Secretary

Sean Van Young . . . Hired Expedition Personnel

Tokilo Karpala . . . Hired professional security
Personnel

Orokuru . . . Tour guide in Africa

Miori . . . Orokuru's sister

CHAPTER ONE

Prof. Kumar is a retired History Professor at the City University of New York. He is a short wheatish man of Indian Origin weighing around two hundred Pounds. He wears round gold framed spectacles and is half bald. He supports a goat beard and has few leftover grey locks of hair at the back of his head. He is always scowling and in terrible mood. He has a dangling cigar which he seldom lights up. He is a ferocious reader and is always immersed deep into fat books.

Ms Erika Trompkova is a blue eyed young, beautiful blonde, Vivacious and sexy lady with a figure of Miss Universe and works as Prof. Kumar's Personal Secretary. She is very fashionable and loves to have fun. She is very outgoing and loves adventure. Her parents came from Russia after lots of trouble by hiding in a cargo ship.

Prof. Kumar is researching secretly on treasure hunt in Africa. He has discovered that in fifteen century a king had denoted jewelry and diamonds worth billions of dollars to a temple as a ceremonial gift. After his death there was a disastrous earthquake and his kingdom got buried under the rubble. His kingdom was near the Congo basin. With time the world forgot about the kingdom. But Prof Kumar has been reading and researching about the kingdom. He has prepared a map and has been able to pinpoint the location and details of the temple. Now he has discussed it with Ms Erika who is very excited about their new adventure of going to Africa to hunt the treasure. Ms Erika was going to get two hundred thousand US dollars plus all the expenses on the journey.

Prof. Kumar has been looking for Expedition Leader and after painful Screening has short listed Mr. Sean Van Young.

Mr. Sean is very talented, handsome, white tall Hunk. He is six feet tall with well chiseled body.

He is a fast cookie and loves fun and adventure. Mr. Sean was Paid Five hundred thousand US dollars and plus all the expenses on the Journey.

Prof. Kumar has also been looking for an African descent who will assist them in Africa. He has been lucky to have found Mr. Tokilo Karpala who is from Democratic Republic of Congo and can speak Swahili, French languages fluently along with the English language. He has a slight African accent. He is tall, dark and has slim athletic body well maintained. Mr. Tokilo is a well mannered, respectable and very humble man. Mr. Tokilo was paid four hundred thousand US dollars plus all the expenses.

Now with team of these worthy people Prof. Kumar is all set to go to Africa. He has booked airlines tickets to Kisangani. It is a city on the banks of River Congo in the midst of Democratic Republic of Congo. He started the Journey on February 10th. After grueling flight of twenty hours with two stopovers in Europe and African continent finally he reached his Hotel Le Chalet in Kisangani. The Hotel is very old fashioned and two storied.

Chapter Two

Kisangani is the capital city of the province of Tshopo surrounded by mountains. It is a tropical city with high temperatures and monsoon rains. According to the map prepared by Prof. Kumar the temple is buried fifty miles off the northern Rainforests of River Congo near Kisangani. Prof. Kumar has entrusted Tokilo to find a local tour guide in Kisangani as Tokilo knows the details about Kisangani and is from Kisangani. Prof. Kumar plans to start the hunt in two weeks. He wants his team to get adjusted to the the new surroundings.

Kisangani is urbanized city with bars, nightclubs, amusement parks and recreational sites. The Wagenia Falls, Kisangani Hydroelectric dam and the zoo are major tourist attractions. Sean and Erika are slowly getting friendly and enjoy each other's company. Tokilo is going round the town reminiscing his childhood on the streets. Tonight he is visiting down town area where most of the bars and nightclubs host live music and tourists flock to them. He has a meeting with a guy at the Le Chic nightclub. Tokilo had been going around the town looking for a tour guide. One of his old friends has recommended a guy and he was going to meet him at the nightclub. The atmosphere is full of ambience and fun. On the dance floor a young couple is dancing to the tune of the song . . . My heart skips a beat ! A romantic song by Chad Dexter. Tokilo ordered a Double shot of Absolut Vodka at his table. He saw a short medium built dark man with flat nose. He was bald and his head glistened in the disco lights. Tokilo had a gut feeling that this was the guy. Tokilo walked up to the guy and introduced himself. He ordered few more drinks and then he began to talk to the guy. The guy was a stammering tour guide and his name was Orokuru. Tokilo invited him to meet Prof. Kumar the next day. Next evening Orokuru met Prof. Kumar and discussed the details of the journey. Tokilo was also present at the meeting. Prof. Kumar was very pleased and deal was sealed for one hundred thousand US dollars and all the accessories would be bought by Prof. Kumar. Orokuru offered to bring along his sister who is a cook for general help. She was to be given fifty thousand US dollars and all expenses paid for the journey. Her name was Miori. The contract for every team member was signed with lot of vigil.

Chapter Three

Today is a great day with lots of sunshine and no clouds. Prof. kumar has been quite busy procuring supplies and hardware. He was with Tokilo and Orokuru in the downtown looking for guns and ammunition. He was making sure that they were well equipped with all the accessories needed for treasure hunt. Sean had invited Erika to the Wagenia falls. At first Erika was hesitant to go but Sean pleaded too much and was on his knees. She sensed that Sean had fallen in love with her . . . but she thought it was too early. Deep down in her heart she was also beginning to love him. Togather they both went to the Wagenia falls. Sean was very excited in taxi ride to the falls. He was very romantic and gave Erika many glances. Erika was aware of his overtures but she ignored. Sean was trying to impress her with his past heroic expeditions. She was getting impressed but she maintained calm and acted cool. In hearts of hearts she adored him and was falling in love with him. They reached the falls and began to stroll around. Sean was visibly happy and he started to sing a song . . . Gonna go crazy in your love! Erika was a little embarrassed and shy . . . but she had also fallen in love with Sean!

After the song Sean proposed to Erika and Erika could not resist . . . Behind the trees they walked and held each other's hands!

Slowly they were drawn to each other and finally they melted into each other's arms . . . kissing each other to their heart's desire. Time stood still and they were unseparated.

Late in the evening Prof. Kumar returned to his hotel tired, weakened and exhausted . . . Tokilo and Orokuru were also with him. In his hotel room Prof. Kumar ordered dinner and bottles of African wine for three of them. Sean and Erika had been sight seeing the city . . . kissing and cheering each other! They were having a nice time . . . In the late night they went to the nightclub in downtown . . . They danced and partied hard. They returned to their hotel and

Sean invited Erika to his room and Erika went on to shower. After shower Erika glistened in pink towel and Sean was completely bowled over . . . She slowly came over and Sean held her in his arms . . . She resisted but of no avail . . . Sean was already kissing her all over and she succumbed to the temptations . . . Slowly Sean lifted her in his arms and proceeded to the plush bed.

Next morning it was cloudy and muggy . . . Orokuru brought his sister Miori to the hotel and introduced her to Tokilo and Prof. Kumar. She was very beautiful and slim lady with a great figure. She spoke fluent English and French. She had dark complexion and brown eyes. Her nose was not so flat like Orokuru . . .

All in all she looked very beautiful and sexy . . .

Prof. Kumar introduced her to Tokilo and asked her if she could prepare Good American dishes?

She was very outright in her response and boasted that she was very gifted cook and always prepared American dishes for the American diplomats at the American consulate in Kisangani. She was drawn to Tokilo who was quite embarrassed.

In the next week Sean and Erika romanced and went to the historic places, beaches on River Congo and points of tourist interest . . . They went to the lovers hill and Sean made a wish to be with Erika forever and love her always . . . Erika was very emotional and tears rolled down her cheeks!

Prof. Kumar procured all the accessories and made necessary arrangements for the treasure hunt. He had many meetings with the team and discussed the details of the Journey. They hired local workers and made plans for the journey. The mules and donkeys were loaded with the accessories. Everyone was tight lipped about the journey and told the locals that it was a great Safari! Prof Kumar laid the map he had prepared on the table in his hotel room. The buried temple was approximately hundred miles from Kisangani towards the north east. It was in the midst of dense rainforests full of tropical flora and fauna inhibited by ferocious animals. Sean inspected the accessories and supplies . . . He added a lot of tools and hardware items. Miori also checked the cooking supplies, dishes and other utensils. She tried to corner Tokilo and he ducked miserably! She was determined to get him soon as she had set her heart on him!!

Chapter Four

On 25th February in the evening Prof kumar had a final meeting with his team. He discussed the details once again and asked for suggestions from the team members. He quickly read about the details of the entire journey with frequent updates. Finally after careful review and grilling questions the journey was finalized and they decided to start their journey at noon on the next day . . . There were Celebrations around and bubbly flowed abundantly. They all partied till late that night and everyone was dancing . . . Even Miori finally roped the ever shy Tokilo to dance with her!

The Next day was overcast and muggy . . . the temperature was 34 degrees. Orokuru and his sister met Prof. Kumar by the river side with the locals. The entire team was excited about the journey . . . even the mules and donkeys sensed the urgency and excitement!

Midst the chants and slogans the team slowly wound its way through the rainforest. It was a very organized . . . the mules and donkeys walked one after the other in a straight line . . . the locals walked on the sides to discipline the animals. The animals were slow as the supplies were too heavy on their backs!

The team marched on through the amazing rainforest . . . It was full of hybrid exotic birds, animals and plants . . . The sun was behind the clouds and little light came through the dense trees. Prof Kumar frequently checked the map to make sure that they were on the right track and not lost into thick dense rainforest. Prof. Kumar finally called it a day after about six hours. The locals unpacked the supplies and helped Miori in the dinner preparations. They cut some wood from the old dead trees and gathered dry leaves to start the fire. The pots were placed on the stones and wood, dry leaves were lit under the pots placed on the stones. Sean had hunted some wild rabbits and they were cooked for dinner. Miori boiled some wild edible vegetables gathered by the locals and cut some fruits too.

The locals gave the team some very strong African liquor which was very intoxicating. Everyone was enjoying the feast and dancing . . . Miori got intoxicated and while dancing she took Tokilo to far end of the campfire . . . Slowly she strolled into the woods dragging Tokilo with her! Suddenly she hugged Tokilo and started kissing him! He was surprised but he liked her feminine touch and melted in her arms.

Slowly she pushed him to the ground and threw her self . . . Getting on the top of him she kissed and hugged . . . he moaned and whimpered . . . After satisfying herself she got up to leave . . .

Tokilo also got up to leave . . . but as he turned around he saw an hybrid Anaconda hissing and darting his forked tongue in and out of his slimy wide open mouth. Tokilo was terrified and Motionless . . . Anaconda had the body of a snake and a mouth of an owl . . . It was turning around towards Miori . . . She was too scared to breathe . . .

In a flash hybrid Anaconda wound itself around Miori and was about to swallow her . . . She screamed and cried frantically . . . Tokilo jumped at Anaconda with a dagger pulled out from his belt.

He courageously held the heavy Anaconda and with great strength unwound him from the Belly of Miori . . . and the Anaconda lashed it's tail and wound itself around Tokilo . . . Who was losing his breath and his body was about to give up!

He reminisced his childhood, his family, his mother and friends . . . finally Miori came to his mind with her Unique love and affection . . . He let out a shrill cry and with his dagger attacked the Anaconda in it's big belly . . . jabbing multiple wounds and blood flew in all directions from the belly of the Anaconda . . . the Anaconda writhed in pain and Tokilo unwound it from his body and stabbed it many times before Anaconda was motionless and lay dead on the ground.

Tokilo turned around to Miori who lay shocked on the ground and was weeping profusely.

Tokilo lifted her in his arms and kissed her. After lots of kissing and consoling her he slowly helped her to gather her strength and composure. They walked back to the camp too shocked and numbed . . . At the camp every one was too sad and shocked to hear their tale.

Midst concerns about safety issues the entire crew dozed off to sleep . . . leaving some locals to safeguard the crew against animals.

The next morning after hurried breakfast of the leftover food from dinner the team started the journey. Prof Kumar spread the map and traced the route with his thick finger. He was happy with the proceedings and motivated his crew with a short speech.

Around noon they saw a rivulet of fresh flowing water . . . Prof Kumar announced lunch break. Erika expressed her desire to swim with Sean. The crew started to make arrangements for lunch . . . gathering twigs, leaves and hunting small animals. The fire was lit and meat was put in pots to cook along with wild edible vegetables. Cassava was milled on flat stones and cooked along Yam. Miori was still under the daze of last night but she cooked lunch with full confidence and paid full attention to the tiny details.

Erika and Sean walked down the rivulet and at a lonely spot decided to go for the swim. Both of them got into their swimming costumes. Erika was looking absolutely stunning in skimpy Bikini wear and Sean was a complete dapper. Both of them jumped into the rivulet and started to swim . . . doing laps and circles in fresh water flowing through the rainforest. Suddenly Sean saw an hybrid crocodile stealthy following Erika.

He took a large leap and pulled Erika out of the reach of the crocodile. The hybrid crocodile had the head of a crocodile and body of a hippopotamus. It turned it's gleaming eyes on Sean and swiftly turned towards Sean. The hybrid crocodile was circling Sean into whirlpools and lunged forward with full force. In the meantime Sean pulled a machete out of his belt and struck the crocodile on the snout. The crocodile was taken aback and writhed in great pain. The water turned red with crocodile's blood and the crocodile turned around with more force. He yawned ferociously and blood dripped from the snout into his jaws. He came menacingly at Sean who picked up a stout Bamboo shaft floating by in the rivulet. As the crocodile came close and yawned dangerously to engulf him he pushed the razor Sharp bamboo shaft into the crocodile's big mouth. The stout bamboo shaft got stuck into the jaws of the crocodile and the crocodile was rendered harmless. But it started to lash it's tail at Sean in a bid to kill him. Sean stuck at the back of the hybrid crocodile with machete several times

And when hybrid crocodile became motionless he ripped it's belly up. The water turned red and crocodile was seen floating on the water. In the meantime Erika became unconscious due to shock and Sean revived her back and pulled her out to safety. She look gaunt, weak and visibly shaken. She wept profusely and Sean consoled her calmly.

Slowly and affectionately he brought back to the camp where the crew was too shocked to react and there was sadness all around the camp. Slowly Miori came to Erika and gave her a big hug. Together everyone ate the lunch which was very delicious but nobody cared about it due to the incident.

Prof. Kumar checked the water supplies and found out that the water was about to finish in big zippered

Leather bags. He ordered the locals to fill the water from the rivulet in the leather bags. The donkeys and mules were fed on grass and soft edible flowers from the bushes. Prof Kumar motioned the crew to get ready for departure after detailed Study of the map. He was tracing the remaining route with his finger. He was in a hurry to go and ordered all to get ready. The crew wound happily through the rainforest and it was getting dark. The team was exhausted and needed rest. Prof. Kumar ordered everyone to halt. He was also tired and hungry. So the crew unpacked the supplies and mules, donkeys were unleashed and made to rest after the fodder was served to them. The camp fire was lit and a wild boar was hunted by Sean and locals. The headless boar was hung from the strings tied to the four bamboo shafts diagonally over the fire. The fire crackled as the oil trickled down from the skinned boar. The locals were serving African liquor and roasted boar to the team. Miori and Erika were intoxicated and danced to their heart's content. Orokuru and Tokilo were also intoxicated and went to the bushes to get some weed to smoke. In the dark night they ventured a little too far into the woods. As they pulled few weeds from the bushes they heard a roar of lion. They both got struck by fear and froze. The lion was hybrid . . . it had the body of a lion and mouth of a fox and it was menacingly licking it's lips. Tokilo wryly checked his gun under his belt. It was always loaded and it was a Wembly revolver. Orokuru was too scared to react but he carried a big knife under his belt for safety. He stammered and Tokilo could not understand what he was saying.

Before Tokilo could respond the hybrid Lion jumped on him. The lion dug his claws into Tokilo but fortunately he had rhino hide jacket on his body. He was saved from the claws. In the meantime Orokuru pulled out his knife and stabbed into the lion's back many times. The warm red blood jet streamed on his face from the lion's back. The lion moaned, groaned and turned towards Orokuru digging his teeth into his leg. The lion's mouth was red with Orokuru's blood. Tokilo pulled out his revolver and unlatched it . . . and took aim at the lion. There was a Bang and the hybrid lion evaded the bullet. It tore Orokuru's leg up and started to chew it. Orokuru was in great pain weeping and screaming. The lion was chewing the thigh and licking the wound. Orokuru fell unconscious and Tokilo took another aim and shot twice at the lion. The lion moaned and fell to the ground with a thud. Soon there was blood all over the bushes and the lion breathed his last. Tokilo tore a piece of cloth from his shirt and bandaged Orokuru's wound. He tried to revive Orokuru but he was unconscious due to exhaustion and fear. Tokilo ran back to camp as fast as he could and tearfully narrated the whole incident to Prof. Kumar who was shaken. Prof. Kumar sent help and first aid kit with locals who provided the first aid and Orokuru faintly opened his eyes. The locals cheered Loudly and put Orokuru on the donkey and brought him back to the camp. Miori was weeping and as soon she saw Orokuru she threw herself on ground and slapped her chest in sadness. Prof. Kumar was also in tears along with the whole crew. He ordered the crew to halt for Couple of days so that Orokuru could recuperate and be fit to resume the journey. In the afternoon after good lunch and lots of African liquor . . . Miori and Erika danced a tribal dance and Erika got high and pulled Sean into her arms and sang a song . . . When I hold you in my arms!

Sean was visibly excited and started to kiss and whirl Erika around the camp fire. The locals cheered lustily and hooted vigorously.

For the next few days Orokuru was getting fit as his wound healed. Prof. Kumar was giving Orokuru strong antibiotics and vitamins so that Orokuru could be fit to move with the team.

Sean and Erika romanced in woods and used to come back late in the evening. On one dark evening Sean and Erika were in the woods when they heard a roar . . . As they looked in the. Direction of the roar . . . they saw an hybrid Chimpanzee . . . it had the body of wild boar and the mouth of a chimpanzee . . . It's eyes were gleaming and his jaws were full of menacing sharp teeth . . . It came galloping towards Sean and Erika. Sean motioned Erika to jump and climb up the hanging branches of nearby tree. Sean pulled out a long sharp sword from his belt and with full force pushed the sword down the throat of the hybrid chimpanzee . . . the chimpanzee moaned in pain and Sean let go the sword . . . the chimpanzee was whimpering in great pain and it darted towards Erika . . . the blood was dripping all over the ground . . .

It jumped up the branches but the pain was too much and with a thud it fell on the ground . . . In a flash Sean pulled out his revolver and shot several times at the hybrid chimpanzee . . . It moaned ferociously and rolled over the ground before becoming motionless. Erika was stunned and too scared to react . . . Finally Sean brought her down the tree . . . She wept profusely and clung tightly to Sean who consoled her repeatedly . . . Sean and Erika walked back to the camp and narrated their narrow escape to the crew and the crew was too shocked and scared to speak . . . The whole night everyone was restless and sleepless! Next morning Prof. Kumar finally ordered the crew to move. Miori was happy that Orokuru could move forward slowly but without any problems or pain.

CHAPTER FIVE

The locals packed the bags and loaded them on the mules and donkeys. Slowly the crew moved along the narrow path in the rainforest. The sky was dark and rain began to pour heavily. The sky was lit with lightning and thundering. Everyone ran for cover in thick forest.

It got more dark and it rained for hours. After the strong rainfall, everyone reassembled at the same place . . . but Prof. Kumar was missing as he had been kidnapped by the tribals hiding in the bushes. The team was shocked and stunned

But Sean suggested to halt the Journey for a while till Prof. Kumar returned back safely. Everyone agreed and the camp was set for the next few days.

The tribals tied Prof. Kumar with his hands behind and forced him to follow them into the thick woods. Prof. Kumar kept noticing the way and made mental notes about important landmarks. He was getting tired and finally the tribals came to an old village which was full of tribals and many monuments. There was an ancient temple and many little huts.

The tribals pushed Prof. Kumar into the temple as the tribals surrounded them and chattered excitedly.

Inside the temple was the tribal king who was praying to God deity. After prayers The king took a long look at Prof. Kumar and motioned the tribals to take him out in the back yard of the temple. Prof. Kumar was brought to the back yard. Slowly the tribals untied him and bathed Prof. Kumar with sacred holy water and many fragrances were sprinkled on Prof. Kumar. Holy sermons were chanted by the king and the tribals danced around the ceremonial fire as Prof. Kumar was going to be sacrificed to the deity. There was celebration all around as the tribals were summoned to the ancient temple.

Prof. Kumar was pale with fright and visibly shaken. Suddenly the earth began to shake and everything was shaking like leaves. The king was scared and the tribals ran out of the temple. Prof. Kumar saw this as his only opportunity to escape and he too ran out of the temple. He ran and ran away from the back yard to wards the open area with no walls or monuments. As he turned around to see he saw that the temple was torn down and all the tribals along with king had been buried under the rubble. After a while Prof kumar regained his confidence and composure as he was too much shaken. He slowly and reluctantly began to get get back to the back yard. He bowed in reverence in the direction of the torn temple.

To his astonishment he saw something dazzling from the ruins of the temple. He summoned courage and quickly reached the rubble. With great difficulty he pushed big and heavy slabs of concrete to the side. He could not believe his eyes as he saw big sized Diamonds and exotic jewelry strewn around the damaged ancient jewelry box. He removed his jacket and put all the jewelry and diamonds in it and the tied it tightly with strings he found around in the ruins. He was very happy and excited. He had erred in his predictions about the location of the temple and had traced a wrong map . . . But God had helped him find the right location of the temple. He thanked God and bowed down in deep respect. Slowly he pushed rubble aside and started to go back to the camp.

He was excited and thought about his crew. He was able to find his way after lots of difficulty and stress. But he securely held on to the jacket. As he moved a little forward he froze as he saw a black with yellow spots deadly Jaglion slowly moving forward towards him. Prof stopped and held his breath and prayed to God...To Professor's surprise as Jaglion jumped towards him a Unicorn came galloping and swung at Jaglion and with his strong long horn threw him up in the air. Jaglion was struck in the stomach and blood sprayed in the air. Jaglion fell with a great thud on the ground. Quickly Jaglion jumped at the Unicorn. Unicorn came galloping fast at the Jaglion and lifting it's front legs delivered blows at the Jaglion. In a flash Jaglion jumped at Unicorn and dug it's paws in the back of Unicorn. With a loud snort Unicorn shook sideways and threw the Jaglion to the ground and delivered powerful blows with it's front legs into the stomach of the Jaglion. Then it pierced it's horn into the stomach of the Jaglion and with full might flung it far away. Jaglion lay dead motionless at the far ground and Unicorn slowly limped back into the woods.

Prof. Kumar was horrified and had too much difficulty in breathing. He thanked God for the miraculous escape and ate some wild berries and drank water from the stream flowing. His strength was depleting but he was very determined as he held the jacket to his chest. Sometimes he staggered and fell down on the ground. But he got back on his feet quickly and marched on with double the confidence. Slowly but with lots of determination he was finally in sight of the camp. He had been able to return because of his excellent memory. He vividly remembered every landmark and milestone along the path. As he shouted everyone came running to him with tears in their eyes. Erika was weeping profusely as she thought him to be dead. She considered him as her father . . . she was inconsolable and Sean tried to calm her down. Everyone broke down and started to cry. It was very sad and that night when everyone calmed down . . . Prof. Kumar narrated his escape from the temple and also told about the booty of diamonds and jewelry to his team only. He apologized about his misjudgment about the location of the temple.

The team laughed out aloud and locals cheered from outside considering it a joke.

Chapter Six

Next day Prof. Kumar ordered the crew and locals to start back the journey to Kisangani. Everyone obeyed happily as it has been an adventurous journey with lots of scares and dangers. On the way everyone merrily trekked back to Kisangani in two weeks. There were numerous campfires every night and the crew feasted on hunted animals and African liquor.

There was a grand party organized by Prof. Kumar on arrival in Kisangani. Everyone one was enjoying the song Sung by Sean for Erika who was looking very beautiful. The song was . . . You can count on me!

The couple danced on the floor and everyone was clapping for Sean and Erika. After the party Prof. Kumar thanked the team and crew for their invaluable cooperation and handed each member mementos and payment checks. He was cheered loudly. The party went on to the wee hours of the night. Everyone had a great time. The next day the team along with Prof. Kumar returned to New York.

www.ingramcontent.com/pod-product-compliance
Lightning Source LLC
Chambersburg PA
CBHW030403200726
48286CB00015B/2785